Black Tuesday

A Novella

Allan C. Hanrahan

authorHOUSE®

AuthorHouse™
1663 Liberty Drive
Bloomington, IN 47403
www.authorhouse.com
Phone: 833-262-8899

Published by AuthorHouse 01/28/2023

ISBN: 979-8-8230-0024-6 (sc)
ISBN: 979-8-8230-0023-9 (e)

Library of Congress Control Number: 2023901719

Print information available on the last page.

Contents

The Gathering Storm

I t was a pleasant Saturday afternoon in New York City. Byron and his good friend John Van Cannon were again celebrating the end of prohibition. Usually, they did so at McSorley's Old Ale House on the Lower East Side, after having lunch at Katz's Delicatessen at East Houston and Ludlow Streets. This particular afternoon they were in Pete's Tavern, south of Gramercy Park at One-twenty-nine East Nineteenth Street at Irving Place. They were having drinks while seated at the table in the front windows, the same table documented as the place where the famous short story, *The Gift of the Magi,* was written by William Sydney Porter, better known by his pen name of O'Henry, some quarter-century earlier while Porter was a resident of the city he dubbed *Bagdad on the Subway.*

'Well, it seems I will be joining academia, if only for an hour or so," announced John, with a slight grin on his face,

"Alright, I'll bite. What do you mean, 'joining academia?'" asked Byron.

"A college classmate of mine, now a professor of economics at Columbia, has asked me to give a lecture to a couple of his Economics classes on the lead-up to the 'Crash,' It's next Tuesday. Want to come along and see if I have it straight?"

"Certainly," replied Byron, intrigued by the idea.

That following Tuesday saw Byron sitting on the front row in the lecture hall, with an audience of young men behind, because like students everywhere, no one wanted to sit on the front row if they could help it; it being the favorite place for professors to direct any questions. Byron was surprised at the size of the crowd. He had wondered how many young men would even be attending college given that the Depression was in control of the nation's economy, even the world's economy, it seemed. And he also wondered how many of these students might later trade their books for shovels and hoes in the Civilian Conservation Corps.

John took his place at the lectern, conjuring up a professorial tone from somewhere, and began to speak.

The Gathering Storm

"The stock market is an indispensable institution of the American way of life. It is a capitalistic delivery room where new business ventures are launched. It is this nation's financial marketplace where investors gather (in the person of brokers) to buy and sell securities. It has seen all the human adventures: comedy and Tragedy, success and disaster, riches and ruin; but it survives. In our noble experiment; it survives, because it is needed.

'When the market goes up some people lose, but mostly they gain. When the market goes down some 'people gain, but mostly they lose. The market has had many upward spirals, laden with profits, and disastrous descents throughout its long and colorful history.

Some examples: In 1869 occurred the gold speculator's panic called Black Friday. Brokers desiring to deal in gold had set up their own exchange and it was on this exchange where the panic took place. However, the violent fluctuations in gold prices had no little effect on prices on the regular Stock Exchange. Four years after that in 1873, a panic took hold of Wall Street causing a ten-day suspension of trading on the exchange, and precipitated the failure of 79 Stock Exchange firms in addition to Jay Cooke, who had over-speculated in Northern Pacific. Some references hold the view that it was Cooke's failure that caused the panic and not vice versa. An Analogy to "which came first; the chicken or the egg?"

3

"Hm-m-m; so far, so good," thought Byron with approval.

"Returning to the New York Stock Exchange, June 26, – twenty years later – we see a collapse of prices setting off a major economic depression," John proceeded. "In the following year seventy-four railroads would declare bankruptcy.

Twenty-one years later would see another suspension of trading; this one lasting for five months, and caused by the beginning of that old-fashioned holocaust known as World War I. This suspension of trading would last from July to December, 1914 and its causes were the 'withdrawal of European funds and the general uneasiness that understandably permeated the financial community.

As we see, Wall Street is no stranger to crisis and the New York Stock Exchange is no ivory-tower institution.

Piecing together discrete events we will try to relate what happened on the darkest day in the history of that institution-October 29, 1929!! "Black Tuesday". Not only was it a dark day for the stock market but for the entire country as well. This was the day of the "Crash."

The stock market crash did not formally begin the great depression of these Thirties, but due to the contrast in the nation's economy on Monday, October 28, and Wednesday, October 30, 1929, and the great impact it made, we can surmise that it greatly accelerated the economic forces already in motion.

Strangely enough, the Twenties began with a slight deflation in 1920 and 1921. In 1921, 171 million shares were traded on the New York Stock Exchange; quite in contrast to the 1.1

billion shares that would be traded in 1929.

After 1921, however, it came to be not only popularly believed but also accepted by leading economists that our nation would permanently enjoy prosperity; therefore', there was an ever-

increasing desire to speculate on the Stock Exchange which developed into a mania after 1927 when up to one and one-half million people had saved enough from their incomes to speculate in stocks.

Looking back, we would be inclined to call it greed rather than speculation. The "investors" (for that is what the textbooks might call them) of that era no doubt would call it a "sure thing" rather than speculation. The latter is a good compromise word as it puts the American investor of that era in a little better light.

During the Twenties stock in new commodities such as automobiles, radios, household appliances, etc., were put on the market. Installment buying was introduced so there was a greater number of articles sold. Consequently, investors began to realize a profit as the value of their stock went up.

This was a general occurrence and induced other would-be millionaires to buy stock. Buying begets buying. This created a "bull market". We know how a bull attacks: by sweeping his horns upward. So it is with a "bull market"; a market that sweeps steadily upward. On the other side of the hill is the declining market which is called a "bear market"; so-called because a bear normally attacks by sweeping his paws downward against his foe. Many investors capitalize on a declining market and turn a profit by such devices as selling-short", ergo the saying: Bulls make money, Bears make money, Pigs make nothing. There were oh, so many pigs speculating during the Twenties.

Many of the speculators who bought stocks during this bull- market" of the Twenties had no great amount of money; therefore, they bought on "margin" which is synonymous with credit and during this period an enormous volume of credit was used to finance speculative endeavors. Many of these speculators bought stock by making a very small down payment or no down payment at all.

This meant that over a period. of a few months many speculators had realized quite a profit, but this profit was entirely on paper for they never sold the stock and realized a profit of cash in hand. Many of them let their greed take over and "pyrimided" their paper profits. They did this by putting up their original stock, which had greater value, as collateral on additional purchases.

This collateral secured "brokers' loans" which totaled $1.9 billion in 1922. During the summer of 129 these Loans increased at the rate of $400 million a month so that by September they totaled more than $7 billion and leaped to a peak of $8.5 billion dollars in October of 1929. The rate of interest on these loans generally varied from 7 to 12 per cent but went as high as 15 percent. The fact ignored by the majority of speculators was that the yield or return of the security purchased on margin was far less than the interest on the balance of the loan with their brokers. Of course, in those days only an eccentric held a security for its income. The increase in capital values was what counted.

This speculation may have gone on indefinitely except that some corporations were certain to fail because factories and corporations, during the Twenties ~ were often under the control of directors and officers who were more interested in making a profit for themselves than in managing the corporations for the benefit of the stockholder and. consumer.

These executives misused inside information that they possessed (an abuse prevalent in the Twenties) and they withheld from public or stockholder scrutiny their dealings in securities various compensations accruing to them, and the transactions between themselves and their companies and affiliates.

Worst of all were the corporate officials responsible for the issuance of misleading financial statements, upon the basis of which the pubic was encouraged and enticed to invest its savings. These statements were heavily laced with double-talk and out-and-out lies; concealment was their common characteristic. When management did deign to publish annual reports or statements of earnings it was a good bet that the statements contained everything but the truth. When these corporations failed, so did their stock.

People who had bought stock, on margin, in these particular corporations found themselves owing for stock that was worthless. Since so many of them had put every cent they had in the "market" they did the only thing they could do to cover their losses: they sold other stock for which they owed. It was akin to a chain reaction for when a great deal of a corporation's stock is sold, the value of that stock oftentimes goes down.

In 1929 ~ when this happened, many speculators would sell their stock immediately for fear they would not realize as great a profit. Selling also begets selling. This increased selling caused the value of the stock to plummet. Then other stockholders in this same corporation would realize a loss and sell stock that they owned in another corporation.

It: is obvious how far-reaching would be the effects of the failure of even one firm. However, let's carry the damage even further by using "pyramids"–an organization of corporations to hold stock in other corporations which could conceivably hold stock in yet other corporations. These layers of corporations holding each other were naturally called holding companies.

By 1929 it was quite common for holdi.ng-company structures to be six or even eight-tiers-high. These financial tenements were extremely intricate and it is unlikely that anyone fully understood them or could.

These pyramids were safe so long as the earnings of the foundation company *were* secure, but if anything happened to the underlying company there was trouble, for it was the practice for the upper tier companies to issue bonds or preferred stock against the stock of the lower-tier companies. Needless to say, these pyramids were responsible for the wholesale collapse of corporations. An unfortunate sidelight is that many banks were committed to these pyramids or were controlled by them.

The small investor–"the little man"–pyramiding his paper profits in the stock of individual companies which themselves were part of a corporate pyramid, contributed to the disaster, albeit he was aided by the corporation officer. He was also aided by some "big league" investors, operating in the form of "pools" i.e., s groups of investors pooling their resources and investing as one–a mutual fund in reverse. Instead of one investor placing funds with a manager and letting him in-invest those funds in diversified securities, we have a situation where diversified investors placed

These pool managers or operators would first arrange for a source of supply of a security, usually through options, and then by coordinated manipulation create interest in the stock to a degree their funds with a manager who invested those funds in one security. that the public was clamoring to purchase it. At an opportune moment the operators would levels to which the pool had pushed the prices were inflated, of course, but as long as there was new money coming in–from new investors–there remained a demand for the pool- manipulated stock. As the number of new customers dwindled there was a levelling of prices. ~Dinking the peak was reached, the capital-gain seekers began cashing in. Without organized support and in the face of this unloading, the prices of these securities would quietly descend.

Under the circumstances, a relatively small downturn in prices was disastrous. There were the familiar sales to meet margin calls, causing more calls and more selling pressures. If the pools had been few in number or had manipulated only a few securities there would have been only ripples, but because 107 stocks listed on the New York Stock Exchange were subjected to one or more pools in 1929 alone, waves ensued, This was to be expected when some of the stocks were such names as A.T. & T., American Tobacco, Gimbel Brothers, Curtiss Wright, B. F. Good-rich, RCA and Safeway Stores.

In a later investigation of the "crash" it would be learned that between January 1, 1929 and August 31, 1933, some 175 member firms of the Stock Exchange Participated in pools, syndicates, or combines. This was not including individual members, nor was it including member and non-member partners.

In a later investigation of the "crash" it would be learned that between January 1, 1929 and August 31, 1933, some 175 member firms of the Stock Exchange participated in pools, syndicates, or combines. This was not including individual members, nor was it including member and non-member partners.

Beginning October 24, 1928 and ending May 17, 1929, one pool managed to present its participants a profit of nearly $13 million, and this with only one member furnishing any money for the purchase of the official. stock. Among the recipients of this bountiful harvest Were such financial institutions and personages as the Chase Securities Corporation, the securities affiliate of the Chase National Bank; Shermar Corporation, a private corporation owned by the family of Albert H. Wiggin, chairman of the governing board of the Chase National Bank; Harry F. Sinclair, chairman of the Executive Committee of the Sinclair Consolidated Oil Corporation; and the ineffable market operator, Arthur W. Cutler, a member of the Chicago Board of Trade. Pleas for caution were called for but were seldom, if ever, delivered.

So we see that even a segment of the press was responsible for the conditions present in the Twenties.

Were any words of restraint forthcoming from that voice which can be the loudest in the land? On the contrary, any time the stock market slumped President Hoover or some high official in his administration would issue a statement declaring that business was "fundamentally sound", that permanent prosperity was now here, or that the present slump was "seasonal". Secretary of the Treasury Andrew W. Mellon, is said to have "opposed all action to curb the boom •••"

Hoover did not become President until March 1, 1929 and by then the collapse of the stock market was inevitable, but strong, decisive restraints may have tempered the disaster. No one can say for sure if even a strong President could have arrested the plunge but it doesn't seem as if Hoover even tried in the six months preceding the event. Also, Hoover had been Secretary of Commerce under both Harding and Coolidge and so was not ignorant of the financial situation in the country.

Hoover's predecessor, Calvin Coolidge, was guilty of "that masterly inactivity for which he was so splendidly equipped." according to the late writer William Allen White, "The Sage of Emporia" (Kansas). Coolidge watched the boom roll along and did nothing to stop it and was out of Office when the boom stopped itself. He therefore escaped a lot of this blame that was due him.

Coolidge took office in August, 1923 upon the death of Warren G. Harding. Harding died owing his stock broker 180,000 dollars—the result of disastrous speculation–but it is a mystery how he managed to lose so much money at the beginning of the boom.

Presidents Harding, Coolidge and Hoover reflected the tenor of the times: optimism and complacency. Strange partners these, but there they were.

Outside of the Federal Government, spokesmen (self-proclaimed or otherwise) for the business and banking community were vehemently opposed to any governmental action concerning the market. For example, in the spring of Twenty-nine there was a voice crying in the wilderness in the form of moderate action being planned by the Federal Reserve Board. This caused a sharp drop in the market. Thereupon, Charles E. Mitchell, head of the National City Bank, poured in new monies.

"He had an obligation, he said, that was paramount to any Federal Reserve warning, or anything else, to avert a crisis in the money market."

In other words, he was determined to keep the boom going, no matter what anyone in Government thought.

John Kenneth Galbraith writes in Days of Boom and Bust: "There were some businessmen and bankers–like (Charles E.) Mitchell and Albert Wiggin (of the 'pool') of the Chase National Bank– who may have vaguely sensed that the end of the boom would mean their own business demise"

Paul M. ·Warburg, called a "distinguished and respected Wall Street leader,", wondered what could come of the orgy but was subjected to criticism–even abuse–for his foresight. He said that the days following his statement "were the most difficult of his life."

Some liberal Republicans and even conservative Democrats like Senator E. Carter Glass of Virginia exhibited foresight and criticized the boom. They correctly sensed that things were going wrong but they belonged to such a small minority.

With so little hindrance and so many unethical (though legal) practices, we wonder how the boom lasted as long as it did. As stated earlier, by the spring of Twenty-nine the crash was inevitable.

It was now just a matter of when and how severe it would be."

"Great lecture!" Byron exclaimed to himself, as John stepped back from the lectern.

As John Van Cannon concluded his lecture, the applause began and grew, while Byron's mind flashed back to that time on which John had expounded.

The Deluge

———⟊◈⟐———

Byron Merriken woke up on the last Sunday morning of October, 1929 with a particularly bad headache. It told him that one, or both, of the two new speakeasies that he and his friends visited the evening before served adulterated liquor, and were not to be patronized again.

Byron and his friends from the Financial District got together the last Saturday evening of every month, except December, to do what they named a "speakeasy sprawl," Byron having rejoined the group after a two-year hiatus because Jeanine had not approved of their monthly adventures in mid-town Manhattan. Jeanine left Byron in July, just after her birthday. He grieved for her, and lamented the void in his life, but life goes on, he decided, so he rejoined his friends, who were Wilroy Freed, Bertram Russel, Friedrich Schmit and John Van Cannon, who if required to do so could trace his ancestry back to the Knickerbockers, when the British of New York married into the old Dutch families of New Amsterdam.

John was Byron's friend, as well as co-worker, but was about a dozen years older and had two teenage children: nineteen year-old-Dolly and her younger brother, Bobby, aged sixteen.

Byron recalled how John's wife, Molly, a raven-haired, blue-eyed beauty, had decided that she wanted to work outside the home when the offspring reached high school, so she colored the grey in her hair, changed her hair style, and was successful in gaining employment at a prestigious Wall Street law firm. And when it was learned that she was proficient in shorthand, the curvy older woman was promoted to the stenography pool, creating chagrin among the young women left behind; them with boyish hips and unaccentuated breasts in their sleek dresses of the latest flapper style.

In time, Molly came to the attention of one of the up-and-coming-attorneys who always seemed to have a lot of briefs and letters to dictate, which he did with enthusiasm, shedding his suit jacket, revealing his bright-red suspenders, and rolling up the sleeves of his expensive dress shirts, to march around his office, flourishing a big cigar, like the powerful, in-charge attorney that he fancied himself to be. And somehow, Molly was impressed by him and his theatrics.

Concurrently, Molly was not impressed with her home life. Her son Bobby was immature for his age, difficult to deal with, and rebelled against her efforts to instill in him her virtuous ideals. John was rather stodgy and inattentive, the latter made more acute by Dolly competing with her mother for John's attention: teasing him and being extremely physical, actions which Byron once observed as bordering on incestuous. Consequently, Molly once left the household for a week to stay at a hotel, to take a break, she told them, but when she returned she was greeted so coldly that she moved back to the hotel for an extended stay.

It took a while, but the attorney for whom Molly took so much dictation finally convinced her to eventually succumb to his personality and move in with him in his apartment in Chelsea, just off Twenty-third Street, a liaison that devastated her husband John, and even more so young Bobby, when he somehow found out the transformation that had taken place in his former Methodist Sunday-School-Teacher-mother.

Daughter Dolly took the news with nonchalance. Now, she would have her daddy all to herself, but she was to be sorely disappointed because to John she would always be his dear child, his little girl; therefore, she took her load of yearning and cut a path of conquest through all the young men she knew, leaving frustrations or broken hearts In her wake, until she met that one young man who possessed the balance of tenderness and dominance that she was seeking, leaving her late one night in an equilibrium bitter-sweet: bitter because she was no longer a virgin; and sweet, because she had experienced her first orgasm.

Byron somehow learned all about John's family, but never revealed how he came to do so, and, still nursing his headache, he recalled the previous day's progression from the afternoon when he took a taxicab from his home in Gramercy Park south to the corner of East Houston and Ludlow Streets to Katz's Delicatessen. He would have taken the subway, but that line was under construction and not due to be finished for another year.

He took a ticket at the door and headed for his favorite carver Eddie, told him he wanted a pastrami with a couple of slices of switzer cheese. He already knew it would come with a small bowl of kosher dills and small green tomatoes. Eddie began to carve and passed him an occasional slice to munch on while he did so, and while Byron munched on the offerings and Eddie sliced, they discussed the stock market. Eddie knew that Byron was a stockbroker at one of the brokerage houses, and Byron had given him a lucrative tip or two over the years, prompting Eddie to add on an extra few slices on his already generous stack of pastrami on the fresh kosher rye, But even so, as Eddie gently eased the saucer in Byron's direction, along with a fresh mustard dispenser, Byron gently slid two dollars toward Eddie, who considered himself fortunate to receive the usual quarter or half-dollar.

After Eddie marked his ticket, Byron went to the beverage for a Katz's Ale, and then found himself a quiet spot to slowly indulge himself, and contemplate the prior Wednesday and Thursday when the stock market shuddered and shook.

It was nearing twilight when Byron paid his ticket at Katz's, ambled outside and hailed a taxicab for the ride uptown to Fifty-nine West Forty-fourth Street, arriving at twilight, and when he exited the taxicab he stood outside the posh hostelry he reminisced briefly about another New York City twilight, his first visit to the City in the company of his mother and father. They were on the south bound M7 bus from the upper West Side rolling down Broadway, at twilight, into Times Square. He and his mother were sitting in a front seat because she was claustrophobic and needed to see ahead. His father was standing in the aisle, behind the white line, he recalled, holding Byron's mother's hand. It was magical to Byron, and while he could take that ride again, he refrained; he was afraid the memory would be polluted if he did so. And when he mentioned the experience to some classmates in college, two of them told of similar twilight experiences. Jean-George recalled his parents on a return visit to France, taking him up to the top of the Eiffel Tower at twilight, because that is where they went on their first date, they told him. He remembered looking at the City of Light all spread out below him in the twilight. It was so beautiful, he said, and then he looked up and his parents were embracing and kissing. After that, he said, he did not see them as parents, so much, as two people in love who loved him, too. And then Massimo told how his parents took him on a trip to Rome to visit his grandparents, and one evening at twilight he and his parents left the antique hotel in which they were staying and walked the short distance to Saint Peter's Square, and the lights were beginning to come on as the light of day faded, and his parents stood with their arms around each other's shoulders, and there in front of that grand and beautiful Cathedral he felt the most warm, safe and supported in his life.

Byron entered the hotel and turned left in the lobby, making his way to the Rose Room, his group's jumping off place, but known primarily as the home of the famous Algonquin Round Table, the daily lunchtime gathering place of writer and poet Dorothy Rothschild Parker, writer Edna Ferber, playwright Noel Coward, and entertainers like Tallulah Bankhead, Robert Benchley, and Harpo of the Marx Brothers. Other literary luminaries known to be regulars were Alexander Woollcott, Robert Sherwood, and Heywood Broun.

Wilroy Freed was already there. Some months before he had asked the server in which chair Dorothy Parker sat, and being told, sat in it himself, squirmed around, and then wrote a note to Parker that he had sat in her chair, and had "enjoyed rubbing asses with her." He gave the note, along with a generous tip, to the server with a request that he pass the note to Parker, who received the note, obviously, because in her subsequent columns in *New Yorker* or *Vanity Fair* magazines, she retaliated the best way she knew how – with words, making "Wilroy" or "Freed" the name of anonymous malefactors. Wilroy's first and last names became pejoratives, a fact that delighted Wilroy, and so he sent subsequent notes. However, so that she would hear it from him first, he informed his patient wife what he had done, drawing from her arched eyebrows and eye rolls, with a lecture that this time he might have gone too far. But as she eagerly read Parker's columns, she relished seeing her husband's insensitive and crass humor drawing such ire and deserved comeuppance, until the morning she was reading aloud one of Dorothy Parker's columns off-handedly skewering Wilroy, and their ten-year-old-daughter looked up at Wilroy and asked him: "Daddy, what's a homo-pedophile?"

At the prior get together of their group, Wilroy had shown Byron his surrender note to Dorothy Parker before handing it to the server, with a generous tip. The note, Byron remembered, read something like, "Dear Dorothy Rothschild Parker, I surrender. You have won! I hereby apologize and humbly request a cease fire. Respectfully, Wilroy Freed."

Appearing a bit morose, Wilroy was not sure that his entreaty had been honored, because another column had trashed a character with one of his names, so he wondered if his note would be heeded. And all the while the server kept glancing at Wilroy, wondering about one of his notes along with the gratuity, but as he placed on the table the small bowls of celery and popovers that the Algonquin gifted the Round Table, the server addressed Wilroy: "Oh, Mr. Freed, Dorothy Parker doesn't sit in that chair only anymore. She has been sitting in various chairs around the table,"

Wilroy, deep in thought, sat up straight and asked him, "What did you just say?"

The server repeated himself, and Wilroy stood up, fished three dollar bills out of his wallet and handed them to the server with a smile and a sincere "Thank you!"

Turning to Byron, he smiled broadly and proclaimed: "She won the war, but I won a battle or two!"

The remainder of the group later arrived, and as Byron anticipated, Bertram addressed him first: "Byron, what happened last week? It looked bad!"

"Well, it wasn't as bad as Belleau Wood," Byron replied, hoping to deflect the question.

"Were you at Belleau Wood?" Bertram asked, and all of them showed an interest now, because they all had served in one capacity or other in the Great War.

"No," answered Byron, "but my older brother was, in the Marines Sixth Regiment, and when times get tough he puts the situation in perspective that way.

"Were you in the Marines, too?" asked Bert.

"No," said Byron. "He tried to get me to follow him in, when he enlisted, after the Lusitania sinking and Wilson taking us into the war, that he had bragged about keeping us out of, but I got caught up in the camaraderie of my college class."

"Your college class?" inquired Wilroy.

"Yeah, on October 1, 1918 I joined the U.S. Army, "for the duration of the war," as a Private in the Student Army Training Company, Davidson College, Davidson, North Carolina," remembered Byron. They sent us to a debarkation port in Virginia," he continued, "but just prior to us boarding the troopship for transport to France, the Armistice was arranged; therefore, we were spared from actual combat, honorably discharged on demobilization, December 10, 1918," he concluded.

"And your brother had to endure Belleau Wood?" someone asked.

"Yeah. He said it was hell. The German supreme commander knew we Americans were in it, and if they were going to win, he had to do it soon, so the Germans made an all-out attack and drove the French back for one of the largest losses in land in the war. The Marines were sent in to stem the tide, and found themselves about to assault the German position in Belleau Wood in the Valley of the River Marne. My brother said there was no reconnoitering, no preliminary artillery bombardment, and once the attack began, no coordination. He saw swaths of fellow Marines go down. He might have been killed or wounded himself, but for luck, and at one time an officer screamed for everyone to get down. His nose went into the dirt as a wall of lead passed just over them."

There was silence from Byron's friends, and Byron then related how his brother, after the war, began studying history, including the Civil War, and likened Belleau Wood to what the Union troops endured at the Battle of Fredericksburg and what the Confederates suffered on the third day of the Battle of Gettysburg during Pickett's assault on the Union Center.

There was respectful silence all around, so Byron, hoping to lighten the mood, asked: "So, which one of you guys took his family to Antibes this year?"

There was general laughter at the inside joke, because just as there were fashionable clothes and such, there were places of fashion each year, and during the past summer the place to visit was Antibes, a city in Southeastern France on the Cote d'Azur between Cannes and Nice.

"Nice deflection, Byron, but you still have not answered my question," said Bert.

"Well, Bertram," intoned Byron, using his friend's preferred name, "I did anticipate your question, so here is my dramatic summary of last week: 'The sudden cool breeze of this storm came on Wednesday, October 23, 1929 when the New York Times Industrial Average dropped thirty- one points on a six-million-share volume. On Thursday, the wind increased and the dark clouds rolled overhead as the market dropped again. The situation calmed a bit on Friday when 5,923,220 shares were traded'" he concluded with a slight bow.

There was a hand cap or two, and a "Well done!"

Bertram seemed satisfied, and probably somewhat vindicated, because he had a few clients of his limited financial advisory business, which was a sideline to his position with an investment bank. He was one of the few pessimistic about the market, and, over the past few months had urged his clients to ease out of the market. He wanted them to bolt the market, but did not want to precipitate selling.

As they were getting up to head out for the speakeasies, Friedrich said hopefully that maybe they would run into Jimmy Walker again. Jimmy Walker, the flamboyant and popular mayor of New York was one of the few politicians who had come out against prohibition, according to Friedrich, a serious drinker who would state to anyone who would listen his views on prohibition.

Byron decided to set him off by asking him: "Hey, Friedrich, tell us how you and Jimmy Walker like prohibition."

"Prohibition!" spat out Friedrich. Those clowns in Washington get the Eighteenth Amendment passed in December of Seventeen when war fever is high and all us boys are going into uniform, and it's then ratified in January of Nineteen when we are all coming out of uniform and thinking about civilian life again, after the wine and Champagne of France, the ales and stouts of England, along with the Irish and Scotch whiskies. It's a travesty, I tell you. And now what do we have? Rum coming in by the boatload from Cuba, tequila flowing across the border from Texas to California, and the whiskies coming across the northern border, in addition to all that moonshine from West Virginia to Georgia, and the Ozarks. What are we prohibiting, tell me? Legality, is what. And now, all of us are going out to break the law."

Wowza!" intoned Wilroy. Friedrich merely grinned and shrugged. He'd given that little speech many times. And Bertram predicted that the American public would finally get fed up with the situation and demand a repeal of the Eighteenth Amendment, that he predicted would happen.

Some of their drinking places were sedate places behind sedate facades, conducive to conversation and serious imbibing, while other venues might be a large hall, with nightly brawls, and a lot of jazz, with confident young women who reveled in being called flappers, spawned by the Great War, when an unprecedented number of young women came to work outside the home in positions once held by men now in uniform. And Wilroy was usually drawn to the grouping of raucous young flappers as if he were made of metal and they were powerful magnets, not to be seen again, and he never ever related what adventures he enjoyed.

Byron recalled all the foregoing as he treated his hangover, and wondered what Monday and the new week would bring.

Monday, October 28, the New York Times Industrial Average fell another forty-eight points with 9,212,800 shares traded. The deluge was about to come.

Because Byron was a utility broker, he was expected to step in for the account brokers when necessary, but much of what was expected of him was information about what was going on in the financial sector, in general, and the market, in particular, and for this he had a network of informants and confidants who shared news, and granted and repaid favors.

So it was that Byron learned that on Monday night rumors circulated around the financial district that certain brokerage houses and individuals were in trouble or were being "taken over" by banks which had loaned them money to buy on margin. These rumors were unfounded however, for Byron knew failures of stock exchange members were announced from the rostrum of the exchange.

Bankers from around the financial district were hurriedly called into a conference Monday night, Byron was told. The results of that conference were observed the following day upon the opening of the exchange

Tuesday morning at 10 o'clock the great hall - 90 to 100 yards long and almost 80 feet high - resounded to the sound of the big gong as it had done every weekday morning for many years. This morning was a great deal unlike the many other mornings however, for it ended the "New Era", so-called by those whose flair for phrases greatly exceeded their faculty for foresight.

The storm broke in full force immediately after the exchange opened. The bankers, who had met the night before, stood aside as blocks of 10,000 to 80,000 shares were thrown on the market for whatever price they would bring. The bankers had anticipated a day of volume selling and the far-reaching object of this huge dumping of stock was to regulate the flow of selling.

Also, J. P. Morgan and Company, The National City Bank, The Guaranty Trust Corporation and other financial interests reduced the margin requirement for demand loans forty to forty-five percent, in an attempt to retard the selling. However, many stocks dropped five to fifteen points in opening blocks of 5,000 to 50,000 shares.

Even so, the hysteria was calmed to a certain extent by the easing of credit put into effect by bankers.

The "call money renewal rate", which is the amount of capital a person must pay on his margin account, was usually announced at 10:40 a.m., but on this particular morning it was announced before opening. The rate was one percent below Monday's rate.

Actions were being taken, Byron observed, and so informed his colleagues, but to no noticeable effect.

By 10:30 a.m., the volume of trading had passed three million' shares.

Pathetic scenes began to take place in many brokerage offices when men and women brought in stock certificates, which represented profits they had derived from the "bull market", and placed them on the desks of brokers to provide additional capital or to be sold to meet margin requirements.

Byron told his bosses and the account brokers to brace for the onslaught.

The sudden cool breeze of this storm came on Wednesday, October 23, 1929 when the New York Times Industrial Average dropped thirty- one points on a six-million-share volume. On Thursday, the wind increased and the dark clouds rolled overhead as the market dropped again. The situation calmed a bit on Friday when 5,923,220 shares were traded. Monday, October 28, the New York Times Industrial Average fell another forty-eight points with 9,212,800 shares traded. The deluge was about to come.

On Monday night rumors circulated around the financial district that certain brokerage houses and individuals were in trouble or were being "taken over" by banks which had loaned them money to buy on margin. These rumors were unfounded however, for failures of stock exchange members were announced from the rostrum of the ex- change.

Bankers from around the financial district were hurriedly called into a conference Monday night. The results of that conference were observed the following day upon the opening of the exchange:

As Byron expected, the storm broke in full force immediately after the exchange opened. The bankers, who had met the night before, stood aside as blocks of 10,000 to 80,000 shares were thrown on the market for whatever price they would bring. The bankers had anticipated a day of volume selling and the far-reaching object of this huge dumping of stock was to regulate the flow of selling.

Actions were being taken, Byron observed, and so informed his colleagues, but to no noticeable effect.

By 10:30 a.m., the volume of trading had passed three million' shares.

Pathetic scenes began to take place in many brokerage offices when men and women brought in stock certificates, which represented profits they had derived from the "bull market", and placed them on the desks of brokers to provide additional capital or to make good losses sustained the previous week.

Byron recognized one of the few women who came in. She was an attractive brunette divorcee` whose boyfriend had convinced her to put some of her alimony into the market, on margin, of course. Byron learned that on her recent birthday, her boyfriend phoned her the midnight before, to be the first to wish her a "happy birthday," and, ironically, to tell her "goodbye" because he was moving to San Francisco due to his employment. But someone who knew the boyfriend well said his job was not the main factor for the move; the City by the Bay was becoming a mecca for those fellows who "play for the other team."

Later, another young woman familiar to Byron appeared at one of the account broker's desk –this time John's – to meet her margin requirements. She was also divorced and attractive: a honey-blond haired woman whose boyfriend brought her in during the "bull market" and had her set up a margin account. The boyfriend was also divorced, and sadly, his wife passed away unexpectedly from a brief, acute illness, leaving him with three children to rear. For help in doing so, He engaged an" au pair," a lovely young Scandinavian woman – with whom he soon fell in love, and married So there stood in front of the account broker's desk another young woman submitting a folder full of reduced-value paper and no companion – at least, that Byron knew of, anyway.

By 10:30 a.m., the volume of trading had passed three million' shares.

By late morning or noon, upwards of fourteen billion dollars had already been swept away in quoted values, and the volume of trading had passed eight million shares.

By noon there was a great amount of confusion on the floor of the exchange. The communication system was jammed with calls and orders to buy and orders to sell - mostly to sell. The calls carne in too fast to be handled by clerks.

Many times specialists in stocks found themselves surrounded by brokers fighting to sell. Very few thought of buying. One who did was a messenger boy for the exchange. It was rumored later in the day that at about this time ·this messenger boy put in an order to buy at one. Because of the great confusion on the floor of the exchange there was a temporary complete absence of other bids, and he got his stock for one dollar per share; stock worth many times that much.

"And I'm willing to bet a hundred bucks he didn't buy on margin," thought Byron.

Despite the great amount of confusion, Tuesday's session was, so far more orderly than the previous Thursday's.

The floor traders in the exchange became belligerent and irritable toward the privileged few who were permitted to watch the proceedings from the gallery. The public was again barred from the exchange as it had been the previous day.

"That was a great decision," thought Byron as he shuttled between the account brokers to see how they were doing, or if they needed anything.

"We need less sellers," John smiled ruefully. "You know, when the market was climbing, all these people patted themselves on the back for 'good business judgement,' but this sell-off is 'somebody else's fault,'" he observed.

Outside on the street there was great excitement since before the exchange opened. Hundreds of messengers for brokers hurried through the streets, and pedestrians were kept moving by extra details of police.

"The extra details of police was another great decision," mused Byron, as he looked out of a window at the crowds in the streets.

A huge volume of credit to facilitate the financial operation of Stock Exchange firms during the crisis was announced; good news that Byron passed along

One of the large commission houses also announced a reduction in the margin requirement demanded of its customers on the theory that the current price levels were attractive enough to warrant such action. And Byron passed this news around, also.

Another rumor went through the exchange after the banker's conference, and it was that the bankers pool was selling stock instead of stabilizing the market. The rumor was untrue, and Byron did his best to squelch it, but well understood, from what he knew outside on the street there was great excitement since before the exchange opened. Hundreds of messengers for brokers hurried through the streets, and pedestrians were kept moving by extra details of police.

"The extra details of police was another great decision," mused Byron, as he looked out a window at the crowds in the streets.

At noon the Governing Committee of the exchange met quietly to decide whether or not to close the exchange. In order to prevent alarming rumors, of which the exchange was plentiful, the meeting was not held amid the mahogany paneling and gold leaf of the Governing Committee room, but in the office of the President of the Stock Clearing Corporation, directly beneath the Stock Exchange floor. The forty governors quietly came in twos and threes. It was a small office; therefore, many were compelled to sit on tables or stand. Many showed the stress and strain of the morning's developments, and their own nervousness by lighting a cigarette, inhaling from it once or twice, putting it out and promptly repeating the process. Soon the room became cloudy with blue smoke and the air was as oppressive as the state of the exchange. The outcome of the conference was the decision not to close the exchange, a fact that Byron, stationed outside, learned as he questioned a few confidants as they exited the room in a cloud of cigarette smoke. He ruminated that he would need to have his suit dry-cleaned now to get out the smell of smoke, and then hurried to tell his superiors of the news before heading out for any other information.

There was also a conference at noon which extended into the early afternoon. It included important bankers and powerful financial interests. Some of the more important men who attended were: Charles E. Mitchell, Chairman of the National City Bank; Seward Prosser, President of the Bankers Trust Company; Thomas W. Lamont and Thomas Cochrane, who were partners of J. P. Morgan; Albert H. Wiggin, Chairman of the Chase National Bank, and the President of the First National Bank, George F. Baker, who joined the conference a little after the start.

This bankers pool, Byron learned, was buying to keep selling orderly but had no intention of trying to stop it. These powerful financial interests had struggled with a panic-stricken public since the opening and had so far checked a demoralizing and runaway collapse of prices but they knew the selling was a blind mass movement and could not be really reckoned with until it had spent its force.

After the conference it was announced by leading bankers of New York that there was a reduction of margin requirements, on certain types of loans, of up to twenty-five percent. This released a huge volume of credit to facilitate the financial operation of Stock Exchange firms during the crisis; good news that Byron passed along.

One of the large commission houses also announced a reduction in the margin requirement demanded of its customers on the theory that the current price levels were attractive enough to warrant such action. And Byron passed this news around also.

Another rumor went through the Exchange after the bankers' conference, and it was that the bankers' pool was selling stock instead of stabilizing the market. The rumor was untrue, and Byron did his best to squelch it, but well understood, from what he knew and read of "pools", how easy it would be to believe this particular hearsay.

The floor of the Exchange was almost covered by now with the litter - wants and wishes of men, big and small. Over these scrapped hopes for the future and dreams of tomorrow walked men on a mundane errand. They were carrying food to the traders who were too overwhelmed to leave their posts. with a curious heel and toe gait the food bearers quickly navigated the distance to the traders' posts. They could not run because it was against the rules. This was to assure the safety of the elderly men present.

Hungry traders devoured the food. Those others whose gastric desires were nil ate anyway. They would need the nourishment because their usual average walking distance of fifteen miles would certainly be exceeded this day.

The prices of a number of stocks turned sharply upward shortly before 1:30.

The following are a few examples. United States Steel common rallied from 171 dollars to 186 dollars a share;

General Electric rose from 214 to 224 dollars a share, and the American Can Company rallied from 115 to 119 dollars a share.

By 1:30 however, or shortly afterwards, the volume in sales had passed twelve-million shares and the loss in quoted values stood well over twenty-five billion dollars.

About this time there was a fresh collapse in prices which seemed to foretell of certain ruin. Would - be speculators, already faced with huge losses, and traders who had survived the previous Thursday, saw losses get greater. Thus, many more succumbed to the panic and rushed to sell.

Many declines reached fantastic proportions, and ranged from ten-to-seventy-dollars per share. During this time of day, pale and haggard faces were the rule in the customer rooms of the leading commission houses. Things brightened up a little, however, when high barriers of buying orders, erected by J. P. Morgan and other financial interests, slowed the selling. John D. Rockefeller did his share by issuing a statement saying that conditions were sound and that he was buying stock. Was he optimistic or did he just want to stem the flood of selling? Obviously, it was an attempt to quell the panic for he certainly knew conditions were not sound. In fact, at 1:30 many stocks had been selling at one-half to one-fourth of record high levels.

At about 2:00, officials of the N.Y. Stock Exchange delayed the delivery time of securities, bought and sold, from 2:15 to 2:30. Byron knew there was no particular reason for this other than the fact that the Exchange clerks were so behind in their work.

There is no report of exactly how far behind it was, but Byron safely guessed that the Ticker Quotation Service was hours behind on transactions. The stock ticker, first put to use in 1867, would reel out about one-third mile of ticker tape on an average busy day. That day it would spew forth five miles of tape, Byron estimated.

Toward the close there was another collapse of prices and ruin threatened again. Various buyers, such as investment trusts, rushed to close the hole and disaster was again averted. During this closing rally, Byron saw with some relief that leading issues regained from 4 to 14 points in 15 minutes.

The New York Stock Exchange closed at 3:30 and when the volume of sales was totaled up it carne to a record 16,410,030 shares.

And when Byron realized that on any day other than the day or the "crash," the average volume of sales was around 6 million shares, he saw how gigantic was the amount of selling that day.

It was a black day for the stock market, but Byron was learning that it was a dark day for the banks also. Many corporations had loaned money to brokers through' banks and were now clamoring to have loans called. The banks were faced with a choice: either take over loans or run risk of further ruin. A money panic and bankruptcy of some Wall Street banks was averted by the nerve of a few bankers.

The story was told to Byron of one banker "who went grimly on authorizing the taking over of loan after loan until one of his subordinates rushed in ashen-faced and told him the bank was insolvent. 'I dare say,' said the banker, and went ahead unmoved." He thus prevented the insolvency of other concerns.

The bond market suffered greatly as did gilt-edged issues of stock. Other stock exchanges in this country suffered also. On the New York Curb Exchange almost every stock reached a new low for the year, or longer, at sometime during the day. In fact, there were two failures on the New York Curb Exchange. The first failure was John J. Bell and Company, which had been suspended for failure to meet its engagements. The second failure was the firm of Lynch and Company. Neither firm was engaged in a general commission business.

The New York World newspaper said losses to big stock market operators were reported as high as fifty-four million dollars, but not one winner could be found. Arthur W. Cutten of Chicago lost fifty million dollars. A few years before he had switched interests from the Chicago grain market to Wall Street, where he is reputed to have made one-hundred million dollars. (A classic example of easy come, easy go, or: "poor-rich Mr. Cutten"). The seven Fisher brothers of Detroit were said to have lost several-hundred-million dollars between them.

Byron learned later that stock exchanges abroad also suffered, mainly because a great deal of American stocks were listed on foreign exchanges. Americans in Paris, London, and other European cities were heading for home because of paper profits wiped out during the past week. Steamship lines reported all accommodations taken.

Tuesday evening, leading New York bankers met in conference.

The senior partner of J. P. Morgan and Company stated that leading New York Bankers were supporting the market.

Usually, activity died out in the financial district after the close of the market, but not on "Black Tuesday". All day there had been great excitement in the narrow streets of the financial district and it continued on into the night, Byron noted. Details of police remained to keep pedestrians moving and to guard banks. Brokers and messengers, hurrying to banks with large amounts of securities to meet demands of the market, had armed escorts. Clerks and brokers, who were already exhausted, worked until daylight.

Some firms engaged rooms in downtown hotels so employees could get some sleep between the time they finished work and Wednesday's market opening.

In one commission house a clerk fainted, was revived, and put back to work.

Tuesday night there was a meeting of the Federal Reserve Board which studied the situation. However, no statement was fosrthcoming.

Officials in Washington still held to the opinion that the "Crash" would not affect business. President Hoover issued a statement in which he said, "The fundamental business of the country is on a sound and prosperous basis."

However, Senator Robinson, a democrat from Arkansas, said that President Hoover encouraged speculation by making statement after statement on the prosperity of the Nation. Thus, he blamed President Hoover for the "Crash.."

Learning of Senator Robinson's indictment, Byron tended to agree that in the light of history of the market, President Hoover may be considered a contributing factor in the "Crash," due to his lak of foresight and aforementioned encouragement, but the manipulation of the market by financial powers and the greed of many speculators will have to take a lion's share of the blame for the stock market crash of 1929, when the Big Bull

Market died, he concluded. And he was certain that Bert would share his viewpoint.

"Billions of dollars of profits," reflected Byron, "both realized and on paper, vanished that day. The butcher, the baker, and the electric-light-bulb-maker had lost their capital, sacins and profits. In every town," he reflected further, "were well-to-do families who overnight became bankrupt or debt-ridden." Waxing poetic, Byron mused: "Speculators...dreaming of retiring young, back where they had started from."

"And it doesn't look like I'll be buying that boat I've been looking at, sailing on Long Island Sound and weekending in the Hamptons," he realized.

Black Tuesday - the name it would later be given - was over.

The" day was ended. A. J. Brown, an economics author, wrote that the "Crash" was depicted in an Eighteenth Century poem:

> *"Crowds pant, and press to seize the prize,*
> *The gay delusion of their eyes.*
> *And disappointed, feel despair*
> *At loss of things that never were."*

Upon reading those lines, Byron declared to himself that he did not think a better description could be written.

Tragically, the first suicide occurred that night, Tuesday, the day that was later to be given the name of "Black Tuesday." The suicide was a commission merchant and his body was fished out of the Hudson River. His pockets yielded $9.40 and some margin calls.

Byron learned of the tragedy as he was registering at the hotel where his firm had engaged some rooms. John and the other account brokers had already checked in.

"Well, for that guy," Byron thought sadly," today *was* as bad as Belleau Wood."

Later, Byron had settled in his room and reading the newspapers' account of the day when there came a light tapping on his door.

"That must be one of the guys from the firm," he thought as he strode to the door.

"Dolly?!" he exclaimed questioningly.

"Hello, Byron," John's young daughter said cheerfully. "Daddy phoned that he was here and I came to visit him. I wondered if you were here, too, and the desk clerk told me your room number. His name is Stephen, and he's a sweet boy. He told me where the pool is located."

It was true that the hotel had a swimming pool next door where a vacant lot had been, and he noticed then that Dolly was wearing a thin robe with what looked like a swim suit underneath, which she confirmed when she opened the robe. Byron also noticed that she had altered the suit to show more flesh than was usually revealed;

a common practice, he had been told by Wilroy who usually knew such things.

"Aren't you going to ask me in, Byron," she smiled.

"No," he answered, a bit curtly. "Did you tell your father that you were coming to see me?"

"No," she smiled coyly. "It will be our secret."

"No, it won't," he replied. "A young girl like you shouldn't be visiting an older man's hotel room, especially in a swim suit."

"Why not?" she retorted. "And I'm not a young girl; I'm almost nineteen, and I know my way around boys."

"Well, you are a young girl as far as I am concerned, and the daughter of a good friend, so if you do not run along to the pool I'm going to phone the desk and ask them to have your father come for you."

"Alright," she snapped, and with pursed lips and a crestfallen look in her beautiful blue eyes, she turned and marched away down the hallway, leaving Byron shaken a bit.

"I'm flattered," he admitted to himself later, "but she is my friend John's darling young daughter. Still," he conceded, "with her pretty face and blue eyes, and her raven hair, and her curvy body revealed by that swim suit, she is tempting, and I am just glad that I could get her out of my room as quickly as I did." Nevertheless, he din not sleep well that night, so the next day was difficult, but by Friday of that week life returned to a semblance of normalcy, and the financial world moved on – but to what fate?

For days afterwards the newspapers would print reports of more suicides.

Byron worked hard during the days, but in the evenings he retreated to the Rialto, and became a familiar figure at theaters featuring the likes of Lunt and Fontanne in *Caprice,* or Helen Hayes in the ever popular *The Front Page,* co-written by her new husband, Charles MacArthur. And on another occasion Byron saw and heard the acclaimed Italian conductor Arturo Toscanini conduct the New York Philharmonic Orchestra.

Young Dolly, the daughter of Byron's friend John, had finished her schooling for the time being, was working as a shopgirl, and had run out of young men to conquer. She was growing less headstrong, was maturing before Byron's eyes, and they were forging a bond, of sorts, especially because Byron had not reported to her father her nocturnal visit to his hotel room the evening of the "Crash." When in each other's company she would sometimes address him in a mock tone of formality as Mister Merriken, emphasizing the "Mister.," and he would reciprocate by addressing her as Miss Van Cannon, emphasizing the "Miss."

The days and weeks following the "Crash" saw the number of suicides climbing into the hundreds.

Reality was setting in for those ruined by the "Crash." At first, they had been in shock, then just a part of a great calamity with lots of company: high brow and low; the class of people most industrious, ambitious and well-placed. But now, there was no money left. If retired, they had to find a job, but could not find one in the luxury realm; they had laid off thousands and contracts had been cancelled. The jewelers, dressmakers, furriers, and steamship companies suffered the worst, first. Then, the economic chain began to lose links: if the well-to-do and swells were spending less money, down the chain there was less money for restaurants, and Broadway and movie theaters, for example.

Jeanine telephoned one Saturday afternoon to see how Byron was doing. He thanked her for her call and concern, inwardly surprised that he had no compelling desire to invite her back, but reassured her that he was fine; he still had a job, because information was as important now as ever; and investors – professionals mostly – were beginning to trickle back in to the market via the brokerage. After the call ended, Byron realized that Jeanine was now just part of his past. She never was clear on why she left him. Was it for someone else? And then someone else? He was good to her, and demanded nothing at all from her. He allowed her to work at whatever she wanted to, for as long as she wanted to, or not work at all. There was no reason that he could think of for her to leave; therefore, as far as he was concerned, there was no requirement for him to ask her to return. Anyhow, he suffered mightily when she left, and every morning looked with longing at her side of the bed, her auburn hair missing from being spread out on the pillow. He did not want that pain again, so he hoped that she never asked to be allowed to return.

The newspapers, despite screaming headlines and sensationalized reporting of the "Crash" focusing on the number of suicides, actually underplayed the ramifications of what had happened. But so did Washington, D. C. President Hoover, succeeding Calvin Coolidge, who had "chosen not to run" for reelection in 1928, had only been president for nine months, so did not bear much blame for the "Crash," but failed to realize its import, and did not exhibit a sense of urgency – perhaps to avoid a panic of the populace.

However, in April of 1928 Hoover, keeping his promise to help American farmers, encouraged legislation that raised the tariff on many nonfarm products, tariffs that seriously damaged America's foreign trade and thus contributed to the downturn that became the downturn in the economy that became the depression.

Byron wondered at Hoover's reluctance to consider the "Crash" serious, his reluctance "to interfere with the American economy," although Hoover did call businessmen, industrialists and labor leaders together for conferences. All the groups promised to cooperate to keep wages stable and to avoid strikes, but Byron and his friends watched as economic conditions grew worse, while President Hoover saw it as only "a temporary halt in the prosperity of a great people."

No one seemed capable of preventing it as the country moved inexorably into depression, along with other countries.

In Austria and Germany, banks began to falter, due in great part to conditions that even Byron's economist-friend Bertram was hard pressed to comprehend and explain: money deposits securing commodities and other non-money assets, culminating in London with Great Britain's suspension of the gold standard, and the final sequence of events being a feverish removal of foreign balances from New York, thus bringing "the world's financial machine to a standstill," it was reported, at the time.

It was a Sunday afternoon, late in 1930, and Byron was home in Gramercy Park, reading a magazine article analyzing the "Crash," when there came a light tapping on his front door that elicited a slight, strange déja vu.

He opened the door to find Dolly standing there, and she smiled warmly at him as he said "Why, hello, Dolly," foregoing the "Miss Van Cannon," and she answered "Hello, yourself, Byron," reciprocating the informalities, and after a moment asked, "May I come in?"

"Oh, yes, yes. I'm sorry; of course, won't you please come in?"

She walked past him, holding a box the size of a hat box, and he closed the door and followed her to the dining room, where she paused, turned and handed him the box, with an explanation.

"Today is my Twentieth birthday!" she announced proudly, "There was just me, Daddy, my Aunt Myrtle – Daddy's sister – and three of my girlfriends. "No boyfriends," she added coyly.

"Well, congratulations, Dolly," he said, with feeling.

"Thank you," she answered. "Anyhow, we had so much cake left over because Daddy bought one for me, and so did Aunt Myrtle, that I suggested to Daddy that I bring you some; and he thought that was a good idea."

Dolly felt confident and ebullient. She was wearing her freshest and crispest white blouse and her favorite skirt, fresh from the drycleaner.

"I know that is very thoughtful of you," replied Byron. "And I think that I have a cake dish in the sideboard," he continued. He kneeled down then, opening the little door in the polished mahogany sideboard, and brought up a lovely cut-glass dish and its dome.

"It was recently washed, and here is a cake server with it. Let's you and me work together to transfer the cake to it.

Byron's use of the word "together" made Dolly feel like a mature woman and somewhat his contemporary.

"Now," he said, before placing the glass dome over it; "I think that is a lovely setting for the birthday cake of a lovely young woman"

The words "lovely" and "woman" made Dolly's heart swell, and she instinctively leaned against Byron with a long sigh and a whispered "Thank you, Byron," but then steeled herself for his gentle rebuke, like the night in his hotel room the night of the "Crash."

Instead, to her surprise, his arms encircled her in an embrace.

He reached his hand behind her head, grabbed a fistful of hair, pulled her head back slightly, and kissed her full on the lips for what seemed like a long time.

Her eyes opened wide; she was transfixed. His dominating ardor was welcome, but so unexpected. He reached out his hand and told her to follow him, and led her up the stairs. She followed docilly on knees weakened by his kiss. He was in command of her now. Up on the second floor he led her to what he called his bedroom and told her: "This is our bed."

"What does he mean by 'our?' Who all is 'our?'" she asked herself.

He swooped her up and placed her on the bed. She lay there, eyes wide open, wondering at his next action. She soon learned when he leaned over her and began unbuttoning her blouse. She did not move.

"You're not protesting," he murmured, and she slowly shook her head to say "No."

He turned her over partially to work her arm out of her blouse, and as he did so he unhooked her bra. Then he turned her the other way to work her other arm out of her blouse, and when he had done so he pulled the blouse off of her, and with it came her bra so that now she was naked from the waist up, her eyes still wide open. She couldn't – or wouldn't – move.

"You're not protesting," he said again, and again she shook her head to say "No." Transfixed, she lay there while he slipped off her shoes, after which he reached to her hip, unbuttoned her skirt and unzipped it, before gently hooking his fingers in the waistband and slowly pulling her skirt down toward her bare feet, and she felt her underpants being pulled with the skirt until she was also naked from the waist down.

"You're not protesting," he said again, and again she shook her head to say "No," because she felt that he was in total control and command of her now.

He came over to her, looked down at her and then leaned down, kissed her on her forehead, which warmed and calmed her, kissed her on her lips, which excited her, and then he lightly kissed each of her nipples, which made her begin to tremble.

He stepped away, and she realized that he was undressing.

Her eyes were still wide open as he arrived on the bed and appeared above her. He reached behind her head and clutched a fistful of hair, pulling her head back before kissing her ardently on her exposed neck.

Lying there with expectation and desire, she wondered if she was somehow in a dream as her eyes began to close and her legs began to open as he descended on her. She heard herself moan, and while they would exchange their wedding vows a period of time later, that moment when they joined together was for her the moment that they became husband and wife.

For Byron, personally, 1932 was a bright and sunny year. He and young Dolly settled into married life almost effortlessly. And Dolly's father was delighted to have Byron as his son-in-law, feeling that Dolly had married well.

By all economic measurments, 1932 was a very dark year. The Depression was established. In Austria and Germany's fragile Weimar Republic, banks began to falter, due in great part to conditions that even Byron's economist-friend Bertram was hard pressed to comprehend and explain: money deposits securing commodities and other non-money assets, culminating in London with Great Britain's suspension of the gold standard, and the final sequence of events being a feverish removal of foreign balances from New York, thus bringing "the world's financial machine to a standstill," it was reported, at the time.

Each day, in his attempt to be abreast of all news that might impact the market, Byron perused the City's newspapers: the *Hearld, Sun, Times* and the *Post*, the latter the City's oldest, founded by Alexander Hamilton in 1801. Thus, he read of the first storms to come out of the Dust Bowl, a name applied to an area of the Great Plains of the southeastern United States, some fifty million acres, including parts of Texas, New Mexico, Oklahoma, Colorado and Kansas. Caused by drought and wind, the ultimate result would be catastrophic loss of top soil and eventual failure of the farms. Byron opined to himself that the dust storms would become worse if not for adequate rainfall in that area of the country. So, it was wondered what the summer months would bring.

Overcast with very dark financial conditions, June, 1932 brought another type of storm in the invasion of Washington, D.C. by the "Bonus Army:" fifteen thousand unemployed veterans of the Great War demanding the early disbursal of the War "bonus" that they had been promised by their Federal Government. Because he opposed the "Bonus Bill," President Hoover assigned General Douglas MacArthrur the odious task of dispersing the "Bonus Army," and clearing their encampment on the Anacostia River flats on the edge of Washington, D.C., which he did with military precision and efficiency.

Byron read this historic episode with some chagrin, and pondered if the veterans would ever receive their "bonus," and how it would affect Hoover's reelection bid; the latter being answered in the 1932 election when Franklin Roosevelt, and his promised "New Deal," was elected with an electoral vote margin of 472 to 59.

The year 1933, when began the "New Deal," was also a year of ending. On February 20, 1933 to the cheers of Byron's friend Friedrich Schmitt, the Twenty-first Amendment was passed by Congress, and it was ratified on December 5, 1933. Prohibition was repealed.

President Roosevelt's efforts to pull the country out of the Depression were not gaining the results he wanted, Byron opined, but the people supported him. For starters, he empathized with them, and they knew he was trying. Economists like Bertram Russell said Roosevelt's strategy was described as 'pump-priming," versions of economic theory advanced by disciples of the English economist Joh Maynaed Keynes, who believed in government spending to get the economy rolling, and then stopping the deficit spending, in accordance with the underconsumption or over-saving theories and the savings-investment theories, where the government needed to borrow money to offset the hoarded dollars and spend that borrowed money by investing it in such things as relief payments and public works projects.

On a cold March workday in 1933 Byron received a phone call from Jeanine asking if they could meet for lunch, to which Byron agreed. With questions on his mind, he worked through the morning, told his superiors that he was taking a long lunch, but would work late to make up for it. Walking out at noon he spied Jeanine right away. She was as sultry and alluring as ever, even bundled up in the coar that he had gifted her for her birthday a few years in the past. The coat still looked good, and so did she, though a bit thinner in the face than he remembered.

"Hungry?" he asked by way of conversation.

"Starving!" she exclaimed.

"Well, I know of a place nearby where we'll take care of your starvation. There were more places to eat around here, but the boom brought so many new financial tenants that the eateries got pushed out. But since the "Crash" that has all changed, so places to eat might increase. Except, fewer people have the money for eating at restaurants."

Going through the front door they entered another world: one of light, warmth, activity, the busy buzz of human conversation and the appetizing fragrance of food: being prepared; being carried out to waiting tables; and plates of delectable offering in front of eager diners.

A young, dark-haired hostess showed them to a nearby table.

"Oh-h-h," murmured the usually subdued Jeanine, her expressive and alluring eyes casting about the place. "I do like the choice you made, Byron," whereupon he smiled and cheerily asked her, "So, what do you feel like having?"

"Everything!" she exclaimed, and then plaintively confessed that she had not eaten since the light breakfast of the day before, and had fought off hunger with copious drinks of water.

"Oh, my!" exclaimed Byron. "Then allow me to order for you," and when the waitress appeared – another dark-haired young woman – Byron politely waved off the menu and told her to bring then both cups of coffee, smiling at Jeanine that she had had enough water. He continued with their order: cups of lemony-chicken soup, followed by a small Cretan-style salad, and then a small filet mignon with roasted potatoes, finished off with a slice of French apple pie, a la mode.

The waitress smiled at Byron as she nodded and said "Very good.," and Byron smiled back, whereupon she headed off to the kitchen with their order.

"So," said Byron cheerily, resting his chin on his lightly clenched hands. "You asked to meet with me; what can I do for you?"

"I need help, Byron," she began, and then matter-of-factly advanced her narrative, telling him that the small company that she last worked for had become a victim of the depression and went out of business. Her attempts to find other employment were fruitless, and she was now one of the multitude of unemployed, except that the bread lines were fraught with danger and ridicule for a woman, no matter that they had gained the right to vote a dozen years earlier, and as she continued the look of anguish in her eyes grew.

Byron remembered from their time together that when she related her problems, of one kind or another, she wanted mostly for him to listen, and not proffer solutions, so he remained silent. She not only had no money left, she continued, but she was a month behind on the rent for her furnished room, and the rent was due again in three or four days, so not only did she have no job or money, but soon she would have no place to live. As she added this last threat, teardrops appeared in the corners of her eyes.

"No problem, we've got this," Byron heard himself saying, a bit surprised that he was saying it, but knowing that just listening was not enough this time, and Jeanine heard "We" but knew that he meant "He" for himself, but she resisted the temptation to overtly express her gratitude, while Byron saw the look in her eyes – and that was enough.

By now they were into the meal, and neither was willing to let the food sit unenjoyed for long, although Byron did tell her in a brief monologue about the family that owned the restaurant immigrating from one of the Greek Cycladic islands as the Great war loomed over that region occupied by the Ottoman Turks who were expected to join in the War on the side of the Austro-Hungarian empire and Germany.

And Germany, Byron reflected, weighed down by reparations imposed at Versailles for the Great War and also in depression was plagued by a demagogue claiming he had all the answers for that country; some joker named Adolph Hitler.

Jeanine leaned back in her chair, drinking the last of her coffee, and displayed that enigmatic smile that Byron knew so well, but he did not know that it was the first time she had smiled in a long while.

Byron tipped the waitress on the way to the cash register near the front door, and after paying the bill he and Jeanine, both reluctant to leave the warm ambience of the restaurant, pulled their respective coat collars up as they stepped out into the cold of the day. First, they visited Byron's bank where he withdrew a sum of money, then visited Jeanine's landlord whom Byron talked to about Jeanine's checking out, and why, and passed to him her past-due rent. Their next order of business was a bus ticket to Rochester, where Jeanine's elderly parents lived, because Byron had gently convinced her to return home, not so much for her parents to take care of her, but rather for her to look after them. Finally, he handed her an envelope containing one hundred and fifty dollars, a sum she initially refused, until he told her it was only a loan, to be repaid over time if she found a job in Rochester and her parents did not need her with them full time. Byron knew how Jeanine's two siblings were, so he knew she would be viewed differently by them if she returned home flush with funds rather than destitute.

When they parted she hugged him tight, whispering in his ear: "I'm sorry I hurt you Byron. I'm sorry. Thank you for forgiving me."

Byron just nodded solemnly. After all, her leaving him had brought him young Dolly.

That evening over dinner Byron told Dolly about what he had done for Jeanine and awaited her response. She said nothing; merely rose from her seat, came over to him and hugged him, before telling him she was going to begin calling him "Sam," for Samaritan. Then, with a twinkle in her eye she told him: "I'm going to turn in early tonight. Care to join me?"